Time for Flowers Time for Snow

A Retelling of the Legend of Demeter and Persephone

 Written by **Glen Huser**

Illustrated by **Philippe Béha**

Music by **Giannis Georgantelis**

TRADEWIND BOOKS

Vancouver ••London

Have you ever wondered why

The seasons come and go—
And springtime bursts with flowers,
While winter's filled with snow?
And brightly coloured butterflies
Spread their wings in June,
Then curl up in winter
For sleep in a cocoon?
And poppies bloom like fire
When barley stalks are tall—
And through the woods in autumn
The leaves begin to fall?
And why the heart of winter
Is deathly still and cold
And plants that swayed in summer
Are grown cracked and old?
Then listen to this tale
Of grief—a mother's love—
And how the Underworld shaped
The seasons up above.

Long, long ago—except where the god Hades pushed up rocks as he shrugged his shoulders in the Underworld, and where his brother Poseidon splashed water into lakes and rivers—all the world was as beautiful as a garden. Even so, people in towns and cities used Hades' stones for paving streets and building walls, and Zeus, the king of the gods, built a palace of cold marble and granite atop Mount Olympus. But the goddess Demeter, responsible for all the greenery on earth, hated the palace on Mount Olympus.

"You can live on top of this rock pile," she said to Zeus. "But I must live where the hills are green, where leafy trees reach their branches to the heavens, and there are beautiful flowers all the time."

So she fled to the lush countryside with her daughter Persephone.

You can never have too many flowers, I say—
Gladiolus by moonlight, and lilies by day.
Surround me with blossoms—the sweet-smelling rose.
Let me walk in the glen where the hyacinth grows.
Fill baskets with blossoms to set by my bed,
Weave a tiara of violets to place on my head.
A corsage on my shoulder, a lotus to hold—
Can that be a crocus with petals of gold?
The language of flowers, let's learn it by heart:
Flowers for friendship—so we'll never part.
Say it, Persephone, flowers, my dear,
Flowers for us every day of the year.
Flowers for us every day of the year . . .

You can never have too many flowers, I know,
Flowers on the hillside, in the valleys below,
Flowers for friendship and flowers for love,
Flowers as gold as the sun up above.
The language of flowers, let's learn it by heart:
Flowers for friendship—so we'll never part.
Flowers as sweet as a nightingale's song,
Flowers for both of us all the year long.
Flowers for both of us all the year long . . .

One afternoon, even though her lessons weren't quite finished, Persephone asked if she might go out to play with her friends.

"Don't go wandering off by yourself," her mother warned her. "You're very beautiful, my dear. Be careful. The woods and fields can be dangerous. You never know when a god who's had too much wine to drink or a pipe-playing goat-footed son of Pan might become smitten with you. Don't trust any of them. They are spinners of tales."

"Don't worry, Mother," Persephone said. "I'll scare them off with flower power!"

Persephone's friends were waiting for her. In no time at all they were combing the hillside for bright poppies to wear in their hair, and chasing each other with long stalks of wolfsbane.

"Let's play hide-and-seek," Persephone said. It was her favourite game.

Hide your eyes, Persephone, hide your eyes.
Hide your eyes, Persephone, hide your eyes.
Hide your eyes, hide your eyes, hide your eyes.

Hide your eyes, Persephone.
Count to a hundred; be sure not to peek.
I know a spot she'll never guess—
See those bulrushes down by the creek.
For me, the goatherd's rickety shed.
I like that hollow beyond the hill.
The branches of a persimmon tree
Are perfect if you are quiet and still.

Hide your eyes, Persephone, hide your eyes . . .

Hide your eyes, Persephone.
Count to a hundred—take it slow.
You'll never find me in the garden bin
Over there where the grapevines grow.

I like the gate by the temple porch.
How about back of the waterfall?
The best spot I think you'll ever find
Is just behind the meadow wall.

Hide your eyes, Persephone, hide your eyes.
Count to a hundred—oh, such fun!
While we are hiding, you can rest
Happy and warm in the afternoon sun.

When she finished counting, she opened her eyes and noticed
an exquisite narcissus blooming beneath a lemon tree. The
narcissus, with its heart as gold as the sun and its petals as
white as the moon, was her mother's favourite flower. There
were even more of them just beyond an outcropping of rocks.
    I'll make a bouquet for my mother, she thought.

After she had picked the last narcissus, the sun slipped behind a cloud and there was a horrible sound, like Zeus hurling thunderbolts—except this rumbling and scraping and roaring came from below. Persephone's friends ran screaming from their hiding spots and raced home. But Persephone couldn't move. She was frozen to the ground.

Suddenly a team of black horses struggled to the surface, pulling a chariot driven by a tall, dark-haired man in shining armour and a silver tunic. "Ah, there you are, my little blossom-picker," he called out, pulling on the reins to stop his team. "The narcissus belongs to me, and anyone who picks it also belongs to me."

"My mother warned me about you gods."
Persephone found her voice. "If you don't have a
good story on your tongues, you'll make one up
to get your way. Here, take your old flowers back!"
Before she could move, Hades grabbed her
and pulled her into his chariot.

Too late, my darling; too late, my love—
Roots have been torn for the petals above.
And Hades will have a new wife instead—
A living beauty in the realm of the dead.
Too late, my lovely; too late, my sweet—
The flower's been picked—so no retreat.
Your lot in life the fates have unfurled:
You'll wear a crown in the Underworld.
You'll wear a crown in the Underworld.
Too late, my darling; too late, my dear—
No help will come from a fallen tear.

By the river Styx we'll honeymoon,
While Orpheus plays us a sweet lovers' tune.
A sweet lovers' tune,
A sweet lovers' tune . . .
Too late, my lovely,
Too late.

"My mother will hear about this!" Persephone screamed as
the chariot plunged back into the earth. "She'll rescue me
and punish you!"
Hades laughed. "She'll never find you, my dear. Never."
But, unbeknownst to him, Hermes, Zeus' messenger, had
stopped for an afternoon nap in the lemon grove. He had
witnessed everything.

Back home, Demeter felt the earth shake.

Hades is up to no good. Men are never happy unless they're making noise or messing up the scenery, she thought as she stepped out onto the porch of her palace.

Persephone's friends were running by.

"Is Persephone with you?" Demeter called out.

"She's probably just behind us," they shouted back.

But many hours passed and Persephone did not come home. Demeter was beside herself with worry. She grabbed a cloak to protect her from the chill of the night, and with a torch in each hand, she began to search for her daughter.

"Persephone," she called. "Persephone!" But the only answer was the hoot of an owl and the whisper of a breeze through the leaves of the lemon trees.

She searched all the next day and the weeks that followed.

"Oh, Persephone," Demeter wept. "Where are you?
If any man or god or creature has kidnapped you,
they will know my wrath. If you have come to harm,
the entire earth shall grieve."

Persephone! Persephone! Persephone—Oh!
I've called your name throughout the night;
The empty day, the long twilight.
I've searched the woods, the hills, the shore—
Unlocked the locks of every door.
And yet no trace of you I find.
What cruelty has fate designed
To take you from your loving home,
And leave me grieving here, alone?
Persephone! Persephone! Persephone!—Oh!
Do they think that I'll forget?
Without you close, I'm desolate.

Without her daughter, Demeter grieves.
The willow wilts and drops its leaves.
Lemon trees wither, sicken and die,
Scratching their branches against the sky.
Mulberry blossoms fall in a heap,
No wheat in the fields, no barley to reap.
For sheep on the hillside, the grass is gone,
Hungry children grow gaunt and drawn.

She wanders, she wanders, she wanders the world.
She wanders the world and can't forget—
Without her daughter, she's desolate . . .

Bins are empty, cupboards are bare;
The faces of parents are lined with care.
Bent with sorrow, Demeter walks
By gardens blighted with blackened stalks.

She wanders, she wanders, she wanders the world . . .

While Demeter roamed the world searching for her daughter, Persephone raged at her Underworld captor. Nothing Hades could do would please her.

How do you court a captive bird?
With a jewelled collar? A gentle word?
With a silver cage and a downy bed?
A mirror framed with rubies red?

Some wine, my darling, in a goblet gold?
Drink it yourself. You're ugly and old!

A shining gem, to pin to your clothes?
You can shove it, Hades—right up your nose.

A song from Orpheus—so sweetly sung?
I hope the old singer ruptures a lung.

At day's end, a kiss—an epilogue?
I'd sooner kiss your two-headed dog.

How can he think I'll be his bride?
An ornament to show off by his side?
He can ply me with music and lovers' chants—
But he'll find Persephone's not gonna dance!

From Egypt, my love, some sweet candied figs?
Don't waste your time—feed them to your pigs.

A savoury stew to make you strong?

Forget it, Hades—I'll not play along.
Forget it, Hades—I won't play along.

He can't fool me. She seethed. Everyone
knew that if you ate so much as one bite
in the Underworld, you would be bound
there for all eternity.

In the world above, Demeter continued to search the four corners of the earth. Months went by. In time, even Zeus, in his palace atop Mount Olympus, heard the rumblings of discontent. What could be happening to cause such a blight, to make his people moan and cry so?

Hermes always knows what's going on, Zeus thought. So he summoned him to the palace.

Good heavens, my lord, the world could not be worse.
I must say Demeter's annoyingly perverse.
She's shirking every duty a goddess should observe.
It's hard to find a thing to eat—even an hors d'oeuvre.
I know that she's your kin, but still you must admit,
As the queen of vegetation, she's really quite unfit.

Good heavens, my lord, the world could not be worse.
I must say Demeter's annoyingly perverse.
To have a decent meal, I've had to hoard and hide—
For a god of my high standing, I'm really ill supplied.
I'm down to my last truffle, and honey cakes are rare;
I can't remember when I ate a pudding with poached pear.

Good heavens, my lord, the world could not be worse.
I must say Demeter's annoyingly perverse.
There are rumblings in the cities, and people on the march—
They're eating their shoe leather and even laundry starch.
I've never felt so bad, my lord, with bringing you the news—
But Demeter's causing everyone to cry and sing the blues.

"But why? Why is Demeter neglecting her duties?"

It had been a long time since Hermes had seen Zeus look this angry.

"Persephone has disappeared!" he answered quickly. "Yes, disappeared—so Demeter's spending every waking minute searching for her. But she'll never find her where she's looking."

"You make no sense. What are you trying to say?"

"Persephone was kidnapped, taken away to a place she'll never be found."

"Kidnapped by whom?" Zeus roared, and his thunder echoed down the mountainside. "Who did it? I'll fry him with flashes of lightning."

"Can your lightning reach the Underworld?"

"Hades! That scoundrel. He knows I have no power below ground. Take him a message. Tell him Persephone must be returned to the world of the living or . . . or there will be no more world of the living, and he'll have hordes of the dead arriving on his doorstep!"

Hermes had hoped he would be invited to dinner, but from Zeus' black look, he pushed that thought aside and took off as fast as his winged sandals would take him.

Meanwhile, down in the Underworld, Hades continued to woo his beautiful captive. He told his cooks to tempt Persephone with trays of delicious food.

Eat a bite, my precious—
You're wasting quite away.
Some dumplings filled with crabmeat?
A bit of peach sorbet?
Some tasty shish kebab?
Or this lobster thermidor?
If it leaves you hungry—
You can always ask for more!
Perhaps some escargot
With fresh, warm garlic bread?
Scones with clotted cream?
Strawberries luscious and red?
Eat a bite, Persephone—
From Hades' banquet hall;
You need to eat, Persephone—
You're not a china doll.
You need to eat, sweet lady—
You're not a china doll.

I won't eat a bite; you can take it away—
But just let me smell that banana flambé.
And let me inhale the steam from the stew,
And sniff that wonderful mushroom ragout,
And the fumes from the coddled cuttlefish,
And the leg of lamb in the other dish.
I'll live on aromas; I'll dine on the sight
Of all that you have cooked—but I won't eat a bite!

Taste this dish, Persephone—
A chowder rich with clams.
Some chicken cordon bleu?
Some yummy candied yams?

Oysters Rockefeller?
Stilton cheese and wine?
Pâté foie gras, Melba toast?
Chocolate mousse—divine!
Eat a bite, Persephone—
There's food to die for here!
Eat a bite, Persephone
Before you disappear.
Eat a bite, Persephone
Before you disappear!

I won't eat a bite; you can dump it all!
But just let me sniff that cheddar cheese ball.
And let me absorb the smell of the roast—
Oh, my! Welsh rarebit with hot buttered toast!
Let me gaze at those cherries jubilee.
Let me look at those crumpets you're serving with tea.
I'll live on aromas—I'll dine on the sight
Of all that you have cooked, but I won't eat a bite!

When Hermes arrived at the river Styx, Cerberus, the two-headed dog, stood blocking his way to the ferry landing, barking, drooling and nipping at the wings on his sandals.

"Down boy, down," Charon shouted as he pulled the ferry boat up to the dock. "What brings you to the land of the dead?"

"My business is with Hades," Hermes answered. "How much for the passage?"

"Twelve pieces of gold."

"Thief. Your price has doubled since I was here last!"

"I don't fix the rates." Charon gestured to Cerberus, who growled out of both mouths.

Grudgingly, Hermes pulled the gold coins from his purse.

Hermes found Hades in the middle of dinner, eating a thick-crust pizza.

"Have a slice?" Hades waved his hand at the pizza. "Pepperoni, mushrooms and goat cheese—it's delicious."

"Uh—thank you, no. I'm not hungry," Hermes lied and heaved a sigh. There was no way he was going to be caught in the trap of having to stay down here forever. "I come with a message from Zeus. He says you must release Persephone immediately. Nothing is growing on earth and everyone is starving. Soon there will be so many people coming to the Underworld, you'll be bursting at the seams."

Hades scowled. "She'll never go back. I've given her gifts. I know she's fond of my horses. My cooks have prepared the most sumptuous dishes for her."

"But you're forgetting something," Hermes said, inhaling the wonderful aroma of the pizza. "Demeter's blood flows in Persephone's veins. They are a stubborn breed."

"Demeter! That witch! She should be grateful that a god wishes to marry her daughter."

"Oh, I agree. I agree. But it could be—and, of course, I hesitate to offer advice to one so omnipotent and powerful as a king of the Underworld—but it could be that you got off on the wrong foot."

"Wrong foot?"

"Kidnapping isn't exactly a tried-and-true first step in winning a woman's heart."

"I'm a god! I decide the foot I'll use!"

"But Persephone is the daughter of a goddess—and only she will decide who walks beside her."

Hades shook his head and sighed. "I suppose you're right, Hermes." He ordered a servant to fetch Persephone.

When Persephone arrived, Hermes gasped. It seemed that she had grown even more beautiful during her stay in the Underworld. She had the kind of loveliness that took your breath away. No wonder Hades was finding it difficult to part with her.

"My love for you has borne no fruit," Hades said. "Pack your things. Be ready to go tomorrow."

Persephone was so surprised that she couldn't think of anything to say. She just nodded and hurried away. She heard Aethon whinny from the stable, and she realized that there were things she would miss. Especially the horses. They had become her best friends.

She went to say goodnight to them. She was feeding them apples for a bedtime snack, rubbing their noses and smoothing their manes, when she saw Hermes heading back to cross the river

Styx. A couple of minutes later she noticed Hades heading down the path to the stable. Quickly, Persephone hid behind a bale of hay.

The horses whinnied with pleasure upon seeing their master, and Persephone peeked out to see Hades stroking the sleek coat of Alastor, his favourite.

The time has come to let her go,
Sweetest maiden that I know.
Hair as black as your fine mane—
A laugh like the bubbles in champagne.
Lips as red as brandy wine;
Oh! If I could call her mine!
Clever and quick and unafraid—
How I've begged and how I've prayed
That she would give her hand to me—
My perfect love, Persephone!
If only she would marry me—
My beautiful Persephone!
My beautiful Persephone!

Alastor whinnied sympathetically. Aethon snorted and nodded his head. In the distance, from a silver boat on the dark river, Orpheus tuned his lyre and began playing his song of sleep.

"Goodnight, my beauties," Hades said. "Sleep well—tomorrow we carry Persephone back to the land of the living."

When Hades was gone, Persephone came slowly out from behind the hay.

"Can it be?" she whispered to the black steeds. "Can it be that I'm falling in love with him?"

The time has come for me to go
Back above from down below.
But can it be that now I find
I'd really like to stay behind?
His eyes are black like your dark hide.
To you, Alastor, I confide
That when he smiles, my knees go weak—
Can't help but notice his physique!
And when he laughs, my spirits soar—
And good sense flies right out the door!
I've heard that love can make a fool—
I'm no exception to the rule.
After saying no repeatedly
When Hades asked to marry me,
Should I change my mind—and now agree?
And true love find, Persephone?
And true love find, Persephone?

Back in the land of the living, Demeter had gone to the lemon grove where Persephone had disappeared.

"Persephone in the Underworld! Who can bear such news," she moaned. "Oh, my darling daughter, will I ever get you back? Will I ever see you again?"

Helios had just begun to pull his chariot into the morning sky. The trees were black and fruitless, the grass dead beneath Demeter's feet.

Just then, a breathless Hermes stepped out from behind a tree. "I've been looking for you everywhere. I have good news. Hades has released Persephone."

"What! I can't believe it!" Demeter cried. "She's coming home!" Somewhere close by, for the first time in months, there was the sweet sound of a blackbird singing. Green began to creep over the grassy slopes, and the buttery yellow of daffodils splashed along the garden pathway.

"My darling child is coming home!"

In the Underworld, Hades pulled his chariot up to Persephone's chamber door.

"Come. Do not fear," he called out. "Your wish will be granted. I'm taking you back today."

But Persephone didn't rush to get ready. She ran her fingers along the edge of a jewel-encrusted mirror that Hades had given her, and whispered goodbye to her pet salamander, who winked at her from his silver cage. She carefully packed a gown spun

from gold thread that Hades' housekeeper had made for her.
She picked up a plump red pomegranate that had been cut open
and left for her on a platter of fruit. The pomegranate seeds lay
clustered like rubies in her palm.

What is Persephone thinking!
She plucks, she plucks a pomegranate seed
And places it upon her lips,
A sweet, a sweet delicious honeyed bead.
Opening her lovely mouth,
She draws the fruit within,
Sighs with pleasure, licks the drop
Of juice that's dropped upon her chin.

Oh no! Oh no! Oh no! Oh no!
Another seed is tried.
Oh no! Oh no! Oh no! Oh no!
What can this betide?

Slowly, smiling, she eats the fruit,
While Hades, Hades waits outside.
And what is that she's doing now?
One more bite from the fruit so red!
Can it be she wants to live
Here in the world of the dead?
Can it be that she wants to live
Here in the world of the dark and dead?

Oh no! Oh no! Oh no! Oh no!
Another seed is tried.
Oh no! Oh no! Oh no! Oh no!
What can this betide?

It took all day for Hades to travel back up to the world of the living, and as he drove, he couldn't bring himself to look at Persephone, knowing that he would be losing the love of his life. But Persephone couldn't take her eyes off him. She blushed to think of the names she had once called him.

When they finally reached Demeter's palace, Persephone's hand brushed against Hades' arm as she climbed down from the chariot—and the thrill of her touch made him dizzy with delight. He did turn and look at her then.

"Until we meet again," Persephone said.

"What—what are you saying?" Hades stammered.

Without answering, Persephone ran up the pathway to her home where Demeter was waiting. Zeus was there too, along with Hermes.

Is it possible to describe the joy that Demeter felt as she hugged and kissed her daughter? Once again there was the

smell of flowers wafting through the windows. Zeus had raided his own stores to provide a feast. Hermes sighed with pleasure as he munched his way through a helping of apple dumplings and two thick slices of peach pie.

"Eat, my sweet," Demeter urged Persephone. "You must be starved after all that time with no food. If I could get my hands on Hades, I'd bash him and mash him. I'd wring his neck and feed him to maggots!"

"Yes, I'm so hungry," Persephone said. "I ate nothing but a few pomegranate seeds the whole time—"

Demeter's shriek of horror tore the air. "No! Say it isn't true!"

"Just three seeds," Persephone said. "Maybe four."

"All it takes is one!" Demeter wept. "Oh, Zeus, out of love for me, make Hades change that cruel law. Let Persephone stay!"

Zeus shook his head. "I have no power over Hades and the forces of the Underworld."

"Then the world will die again," Demeter shrieked. "For every day my darling daughter is gone, the greenery of the world shall blacken and die as it has these past months. I have power too—the power to turn your earth into a grave! Hades might as well rule in your place! Oh, Persephone, how could you fail me so?"

Zeus glowered at Persephone. "Women—all they bring is woe," he muttered. "Hermes, take a message to Hades—tell him we wish to meet with him."

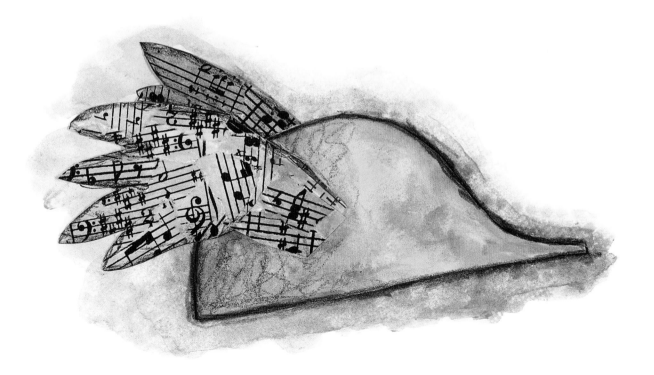

Hermes groaned. Not another trip to the Underworld! He snatched a few more apple dumplings to sustain him on the journey.

In a rage, Demeter hurried from the room.

Take away my daughter
And winter I will bring.
Flowers will drop; corn will die
And birds will cease to sing.
Banish my Persephone
To that Underworld domain,
Grapes will wither on the vine
And frost will freeze the grain.
Instead of apple blossoms
The only white you'll see
Is snow along the branches
Of the barren apple tree.
Take the idol of my eye
And make her live below,
And winds will howl all day long
And nothing here will grow!

Following Demeter, Persephone heard the threats her sorrowing mother made.

"Don't despair." Persephone tried to comfort Demeter. "I have a plan that I think will work if Hades truly loves me."

"But that's the problem. He loves you. He'll keep you prisoner in the Underworld forever."

"Trust me," Persephone said. "I've learned to play the games of the gods."

Hermes was in such a bad mood when he reached the Underworld that when Cerberus growled at him, he bopped him on both snouts and sent him yelping on his way. He gave Charon counterfeit coins for his passage and deliberately rocked the ferry boat as he was getting out, so that Charon nearly fell into the river Styx.

"What brings you?" Hades asked.

Hermes delivered his message, and before he had a chance to catch his breath, Hades had pushed him into his chariot and they were galloping up to the world again.

Persephone met him at the door. She was wearing the dress of gold that Hades had given her, and jewels from the Underworld glittered in her hair.

"She is yours," Zeus said. "I give her to you in marriage."

"I go with you most willingly." Persephone gazed into her lover's eyes. "But I do beg one favour."

"If it is within my power to give it to you." Hades held out an open hand to his sweetheart.

Demeter's hand flew to her breast, as if she were afraid her heart would stop.

Hermes rolled his eyes and grabbed a chicken drumstick to gnaw on.

I know that I have tasted
Forbidden fruit for me,
If I desire to live amid
The earth's sweet greenery.
So I'm torn, my darling—
I'll be your willing bride,
Live within the Underworld
And be there by your side.
A month for every seed
I'll be your loving queen—
If I can visit up above
For the time that's in-between.

Agreed. But I will miss you
When you are gone away.
Every minute, I believe,
Will seem like one long day.
A grateful earth will thank you
For Demeter's peace of mind—
Just promise me when you descend,
My mother-in-law will stay behind!

And so with this lovers' pledge
The seasons came to be.
In spring, the seedlings sprout,
Blossoms grace the lemon tree.
Summer fills its gardens
With food to eat for all.
Harvest comes by waning light
As leaves begin to fall.

The magic circle, magic circle, magic circle,
The magic circle of birth and death.
A time for flowers, and a time for snow.
A time for flowers, and a time for snow . . .

And then we watch Persephone
Go back to her love below.
Demeter withers the autumn vines
And winter winds begin to blow.
Missing her child, the mother mourns—
The earth is cold and dark
Until Persephone's return
Is harkened by a lark.
And then Demeter smiles.
And things begin again to grow.

The magic circle, magic circle, magic circle,
The magic circle of birth and death.
A time for flowers, and a time for snow.
A time for flowers, and a time for snow . . .

A time for flowers, and a time for snow

Glen Huser is a recipient of the Governor General's Award and the Mr. Christie's Silver Award. He has written many books for children and young adults, including *The Runaway* for Tradewind Books. He lives in Vancouver.

Philippe Béha is an internationally acclaimed artist and two-time recipient of the Governor General's Award. He was recently nominated by IBBY Canada for the prestigious Hans Christian Andersen Award for his outstanding contribution to children's literature. He has illustrated over 175 books for children, including *The King has Goat Ears* for Tradewind Books. He lives in Montreal.

Giannis Georgantelis has composed and arranged music for theatrical plays, multimedia projects, festivals and musical ensembles. His two previous children's operas received great critical acclaim. He lives in Athens, Greece.

Chroma Musika (DEKA 2010 & NEPMCC awards) was founded by Greek-Canadian opera singers Maria Diamantis and Dimitris Ilias. Their work has promoted high quality music activities for Canadian children, families, local communities as well as the general public. Chroma Musika's discography includes two CDs and four children's operas with accompanying picture books and CDs. Maria and Dimitris live in Montreal.

AUDIO CD

Cast

NARRATOR
Terry Jones

DEMETER
Maria Diamantis

HADES
Dimitris Ilias

PERSEPHONE
Elie Manousakis

HERMES
Xavier Gray

ZEUS
Terry Jones

CHARON
Terry Jones

CHEF
Jean Philippe Carlot

COOKS
Marialena Spinoula
Makis Papagavriil
Giannis Georgantelis
Apostolos Kaltsas
Nikos Psarianos

Production

MUSIC/ ORCHESTRATION
Giannis Georgantelis

MUSICAL PRODUCTION
Chroma Musika & Panarmonia Atelier Musical

EDUCATIONAL DIRECTION
Panarmonia Atelier Musical

MUSICAL AND VOCAL DIRECTION
Maria Diamantis & Dimitris Ilias

ORCHESTRAL SCORE
Giannis Georgantelis

ORCHESTRAL SCORE CONSULTANT
Nikos Psarianos

ASSOCIATE VOCAL DIRECTOR
Marialena Spinoula

RECORDING-MIXING OF ORCHESTRA AND CHORUS
Dr. Mark Corwin (Montreal)

RECORDING OF TERRY JONES
Andre Jacquemin-Redwood Studios (London)

RECORDING OF SOLOISTS
Dimitris Ilias-Chroma Musika (Montreal)

FINAL MIX - MASTERING
Kostas Parisis-Studio Praxis (Athens)

DOCUMENTARY
Raphael Katz

RECORDING LOCATIONS
Redwood Studios (London)
Studio Praxis (Athens)
Oscar Peterson Concert Hall (Montreal)
Chroma Musika (Montreal)
Vanier College Auditorium (Montreal)

Choirs

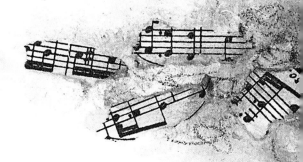

Gardenview Elementary School Choir

GRADE 3 Alexandra Rose Cullen, Alyssa Mirarchi, Christie Spiroulias, Demetra Malaperdas, Emily Santillo, Frida Caporicci Huerta, Isaac Aizanman, Jasmine Pelletier, Malena Di Pastena, Maria Yuni Valerio, Maria-Amalia Babalis, Miranda La Monaca, Nadia Malik, Sabrina Morelli, Sacha Denbow, Sofia Iarocci, Victoria Fidas

GRADE 4 Amanda Lisi, Ariella Caporicci, Cassidy Gonzalez, Divya Kakkar, Elizabeth Bohbot, Ella Parravano, Emma Dankoff, Helena Marek, Julianne Fournier, Lacey Baillairgé, Meagan Lamontagne, Mia Gaudet, Michael Lallani, Mya Parravano, Noa Goldberg, Peter Goudreau, Rebecca Mazza-Lihnakis, Isabella Leo, Serena Duperron, Stefania Korizis, Teah Parravano, Vanessa Dangelas

GRADE 5 Adrianna Ford-Scantlebury, Alessia Del Torto, Alexa Shlien, Anais Silva-Juul, Anna Kanellakos, Annika Godfrey, Charlotte Rose Lavoie Auspert, Chrysoula Fidas, Daniel Bohbot, Darina Diavatopoulos, Efrosini Malaperdas, Elizabeth El–Zawahri, Emma Biello, Emma Rodriguez, Gabrielle Cartier, Gabrielle Decelles, Jianna Christalers, Kareena Patel, Kristina Fragias, Maria Tsoukalas, Melina Di Criscio, Mysha Khan, Panagiota Skokos, Rianna Angelopoulos, Rose Boisvert, Sara Malik, Victoria Anson, Victoria Ntinas

GRADE 6 Alexandra Papadopoulos, Bianca Giglio, Chrisoula Gasparatos, Constantina Malaperdas, Diana Aravantinos, Gabrielle Khabie, Grace Mourelatos, Irene Anoussos, Jessica Langevin-Bouthillier, Khara Lapommeray, Megan Esposito, Nicole Vamvakas, Siona Nazarian, Skye Gaudet, Vassilios Iliopoulos, Vassiliki Gicopoulos, Victoria Douan, Zoe Mikas

Socrates and Demosthenes Elementary Schools

Stella Eleftheriotis, Victoria Mavroudis, Nektarios Psillos, Pamela Papapanos, Julia Stavrinidis, Alexandra Bakopanos, Anastasia Crilis, Anastasia Georgiakakis, Sarah Ashley Ginocchio, Isabella Maria Papagiannis, Elisabeth Maria Dionatos, Anna Marie Karounis Dwarka, Denise Economides, Georgia Avgoustis, Olivia Ambrosone, Dimitra Louloudakis, Panagiotis Louloudakis, Eloise Fyrigos, Alexandra Papapostolou, Christina Polichronopoulos, Angelica Labropoulos, Katerina Papadakis, Andreana Theodoropoulos, Ioanna Tountas, Ioanna Kekos, Elizabeth Kekos, Dimitra Pierson, Elena Hadsipantelis, Danhae Hughes, Violetta Moutzouridis, Eugenia Moutzouridis, Melyna Pavlatos

Pierre de Coubertin Elementary School Glee Club

Veronica Sandoval, Emma Pomponi, Mara Tartamella, Lana Ortiz, Loïce Valery Dikanga Mopena, Krista DiPietrantonio, Vanessa Rossi, Sofia Maria Della Valle, Alessia Vigna, Athena Di Fruscia, Luca Morgante, Alexandra Giotsalitis, Isabella Del Grosso, Emily Alvaro, William Antioco-Neves, Sabrina Ciarrocchi, Marisa Mitchell, Alexia Mucciacciaro, Giulia Gallo, Samantha Romano, Enrique Capece, Sarah Mucci, Isabella Romeo, Pamela Insogna, Nuria Del Busso, Vanessa DiPietrantonio, Zachary Antioco-Neves, Valentina Tsilimidos

The Sinclair Laird Elementary School Glee Club

Sarena Biancardi-Maffei, Lydia Ponniah, Maviley Mantey-Annor, Sienna Bombo, Ariane-Irene Leblanc, Zaima Zubaida, Säsha Walker-Clément, Krishne Selvarajah, Fabrizio Trocchia, Amina Masood, Ummatuz Sabiha Chowdhury, Krishath Selvaratah, Kristen Scolieri, Hayley Harrison, Kaila Walker-Clément, Evan Dimos, Mahua Nath, Sakanah Dharmalingam, Deborah Bemah, Herjuno Wicaksono

High School Harmony Group

Peggy Koroneos, Maria Anoussos, Nikoletta Diamantopoulos, Andreana Moulinos, Marilena Papadopoulos, Zoe Knox, Georgia Baloukas, Tatiana Bogosian, Paulina Moulinos, Juliana Theodoropoulos, Fotini Bizogias, Natassa Lambrou, Eliana Lambrou, Nicoletta Athanasopoulos, Nicky Papagiannakis, Vickie Pavlatos, Christina Di Donato, Nafsika Baloukas

Choral Soloists and Section Leaders

Vanessa DiPietrantonio, Nafsika Baloukas, Georgia Baloukas, Sakanah Dharmalingam, Zoe Mikas, Siona Nazarian, Irene Anoussos, Pamela Papapanos, Anastasia Georgiakakis, Alexis Dimopoulos-L'Ecuyer

SUPPLEMENTARY VOICES Ioannis Pappadopoulos, Sienna Bombo, Fabrizio Trocchia, Alexis Dimopoulos-L'Ecuyer, Stevie Tsoukalas

SUPPLEMENTARY HARMONY LINES Alexandra Papadopoulos, Bianca Giglio, Chrisoula Gasparatos, Constantina Malaperdas, Diana Aravantinos, Grace Mourelatos, Irene Anoussos, Jessica Langevin-Bouthillier, Khara Lapommenay, Nicole Vamvakas, Siona Nazarian, Vasilios Iliopoulos, Vassiliki Gicopoulos, Victoria Douan, Zoe Mikas

AUDIO CD

The Orchestre Symphonique Pop de Montréal

CONDUCTOR
Alain Cazes

FIRST VIOLINS
François Ouimet (Concertmaster)**, Kim Lyth, Anne-Isabelle Bourdon, Nadine Guénette, Tina Becker**

SECOND VIOLINS
Fanny Bulard, Gwendolyne Krasnicki, Nadege Wary

VIOLAS
Caroline Neault, Jennie Ferris, Andrea Loach

CELLOS
Karine Bouchard, Carole Larocque, Vincent De Groot

DOUBLE BASSES
Jordan Miller, Timothy Vuksic

FLUTE
Michelle Moreau

CLARINET
Emmanuelle Guay Da Silva

OBOE
Keiko Otani

BASSOON
Linda Rand

FRENCH HORNS
Cécile Le Cardinal, Sarah Joyal

TRUMPETS
Francis Pigeon, Mireille Tardif

TROMBONES
François Lefebvre, David Leroux (Bass)

TUBA
Simon Deschênes

HARP
Suzanne Berthiaume

PIANO
Hélène Carrière

TIMPANI
Lanny Levine

PERCUSSION
Stéphane Savaria (Drumset)**, Martin-Paul Beaulieu** (Keyboards)**, Lucy Chen** (Accessories)

MUSIC LIBRARIAN
Caroline Neault

FOUNDER AND CEO
Stéphane Savaria
VICE-PRESIDENT & TECHNICAL DIRECTOR
Hugues Morissette
VICE-PRESIDENT ASSISTANT
Geneviève Lanouette
TREASURER ASSISTANT
Hélène Bellemare

Musicians - Athens

ACCORDION, PERCUSSION AND SYNTHESIZER, GUITAR SOUNDS, SOUND EFFECTS
Giannis Georgantelis
GUITAR & PERCUSSION
Makis Papagavriil
ELECTRIC BASS
Apostolos Kaltsas

Chroma Musika and Panarmonia Atelier Musical wish to thank the following sponsors, partners and individuals for their immense support.

Partners

Programme Montréal Interculturel (PMI) – 2013
Ville De Montréal – Direction de la diversité sociale
The Hellenic Community of Greater Montreal
English Montreal School Board
AHEPA Canada
Gardenview Elementary Home and School Association
Pierre de Coubertin Elementary School

Sponsors

DIAMOND CIRCLE
Au Vieux Duluth Restaurants
LANVAC Surveillance – John & Bill in memory of our dad George Georgoudes.
Santorini Bijouterie – Razmick Nazarian
Park Ex Flower Shop - Aris Mitropoulos

PLATINUM CIRCLE
Nick Papapanos - Vice President, Senior Investment Advisor - Cannacord Wealth Management
Spiros Kondonis - Executive vice president and CFO – Recochem Inc
Manu Kakkar, BSc. (Hons), MTax, TEP, CPA, CA, - President – Manu Kakkar CPA Inc.
CKameleon Marketing & Events - Constance Karvelas

GOLD CIRCLE
Andre Michalopoulos - Andion Financial
Andy Crilis & Chris Mellidis - Service de Ventilation Sécurité Inc.
Basil Papaevagelou, M.B.A. - Investment Advisor - RBC Dominion Securities Inc.
Brian Tracey - Branch Manager - TD Canada Trust
Caroll Zeliniotis - Mobile Mortgage Specialist - RBC Royal Bank
George Diamantopoulos – Plomberie Claude Limoges
George Tsitouras CA – Partner – Ernst & Young
East Side Mario's – Chris & Peter Prattas
John Theodosopoulos OAQ, MBA, LEED GA – President - ECODOMUS Construction Inc.
Location de Linge Olympique Ltée - Xenos & Potamitis Families
Madisons New York Grill & Bar
Marco Pomponi – Consultant – Genatec Business Solutions
Mrs. Angelique Kyrtatas
Norm Goldberg – Training Director/Co-owner – Urgences Reanimation
Olga Kalogiannis & Frank Di Fruscia
Sam Scalia, MBA – President – Samcon
Scotiabank
Tellides & Deros - Groupe Sutton – Excellence Inc. Real Estate Agency
Tola Roofing

HOSPITALITY SPONSORS
Mythos Ouzeri Estiatorio Restaurant – Dimitris Galanis & Fanny Galanis
Restaurant Elounda - Bobby Michailidis
Joey's Limousine – Joey Fumo & Christina Maroudas

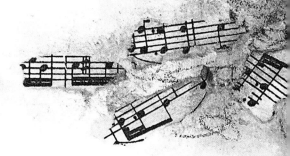

Media Partners

The Greek-Canadian News (TA NEA); Park-Ex News; Laval News; CFMB 1280 AM Radio Montreal; Laval Families Magazine; Edo Montreal

Government Liaisons

Senator Leo Housakos; Senator Pana Papas Merchant; Hon. Gerry Sklavounos (MNA for Laurier Dorion); **Mary Deros** (City Councillor and member of the exec. com. City of Montreal); **Basil Angelopoulos** (City Councillor - City of Laval); **Mr. Nicholas Katalifos**

Under the Auspices of:

The Government of Canada, The Government of Quebec, The City of Montreal, The City of Laval, The Embassy of Greece to Canada (His Excellency Eleutherios Anghelopoulos, Ambassador), The Embassy of Canada to Greece, The General Consulate of Greece to Montreal (His Excellency Thanos Kafopoulos, Consul General)

Special Thanks to:

Senator Leo Housakos, Senator Pana Pappas-Merchant, the Hon. Gerry Sklavounos (MNA for Laurier Dorion), Mary Deros (City Councillor and member of the exec. committee City of Montreal), Basil Angelopoulos (City Councillor - City of Laval), Nicholas T. Pagonis (President Hellenic Community of Greater Montreal), George Vassilas (President, AHEPA Canada), Chris Adamopoulos (General Dir. Socrates and Demosthenes Schools), George Tsantrizos, Christine Long (CTV News), Fadima Diallo, Evelyne Alfonsi, Nicholas Katalifos, Viola Vathilakis, Sandra Leveillé, Sonia Marotta, Hélène Diguer, Michael Tellides, Luigi Morabito, George Guzmas, John Coconas, Joel Ceausu of The Suburban, Claudia del Basso, Andre Knox, George Moulinos, Diane Lacombe, Robin Russel, John Louloudakis, Marianna Manolis, Scores (St-Leonard), Helen Kalipolidis, Joanne Tzintis, Soula Tellides, Carol Deros, George Tellides, Connie Di Iorio, Georgia Chatzidakis, Rania Letsas, Cathy Parashis, Sandra Modonese, Charlotte Costigan, Maria D'Alessio, Angela Iliopoulos, Yota Kerasiotis, Peter Malaperdas, Susan Chomar, Dimitra Demerson, Lisa Fong, Sandra Peruz, the Ilias & Diamantis Families, Olga Kalogiannis, Carla Torre, Niki Xenos, Bessy Bitzas, Irene Michelakis, Carmie Leo, Tracy Mitchell, Isabella Antioco, Caecilia Widati, Daniel Smajovits, Vickie Londos, Constance Karvelas, the Walker-Clément family, Maria Nanas, Billy Balabanos, Justine Frangouli-Argyri and all the families of our young songbirds for their dedication.

Time for Flowers Time for Snow

CD Tracks

1. *Seasons*
2. *Leaving Mount Olympus* (narration)
3. *You Can Never Have Too Many Flowers*
4. *Out to Play* (narration)
5. *Hide-and-Seek*
6. *Persephone Kidnapped!* (narration)
7. *Too Late*
8. *Demeter's Search* (narration)
9. *I Call Your Name*
10. *Desolate*
11. *No Pleasing Persephone* (narration)
12. *Courtship Dialogue*
13. *Hermes Summoned* (narration)
14. *Hermes' Lament*
15. *Hermes Visits the Underworld* (narration)
16. *Too Many Cooks*
17. *Convincing Hades* (narration)
18. *Stable Serenades*
19. *Underworld Goodbyes* (narration)
20. *Pomegranate Song*
21. *Back Home* (narration)
22. *Demeter's Rage*
23. *The Betrothal* (narration)
24. *Lovers' Pledge*
25. *Time for Flowers, Time for Snow*

Published by Tradewind Books in 2013. Text copyright © 2013 Glen Huser. Illustrations copyright © 2013 Philippe Béha. Music copyright © Chroma Musika & Giannis Georgantelis. All rights reserved. No part of this publication or CD may be reproduced, stored in a retrieval system or transmitted, in any form or by any means, without the prior written permission of the publisher or, in the case of photocopying or other reprographic copying, a license from Access Copyright, Toronto, Ontario. The right of Glen Huser, Philippe Béha and Giannis Georgantelis to be identified as the author, the illustrator and composer of this work has been asserted by them in accordance with the Copyright, Design and Patents Act 1988.

Book design by Elisa Gutiérrez

The type is set in Grenale. Title type is Honeydukes.

10 9 8 7 6 5 4 3 2 1

Printed and bound in Korea in August 2013 by Sung In Printing Company.

The publisher wishes to thank Elsa Delacretaz for her French translation of the text.

. . . .

LIBRARY AND ARCHIVES CANADA CATALOGUING IN PUBLICATION

Huser, Glen, 1943-, author
  Time for flowers, time for snow / Glen Huser ; illustrated by Philippe Béha ; music by Giannis Georgantelis.

To be accompanied by a compact disc of the opera composed by Giannis Georgantelis (story and lyrics by Glen Huser), performed by the Orchestre symphonique pop de Montréal and narrated by Terry Jones.
For children.
ISBN 978-1-896580-26-5

  1. Persephone (Greek deity)--Juvenile fiction. 2. Operas--Juvenile--Librettos. I. Béha, Philippe, illustrator II. Georgantelis, Giannis-, composer III. Jones, Terry, 1942 IV. Title.

L50.H969T58 2013   j782.1026'8   C2013-902656-8

. . . .

The publisher thanks the Government of Canada and Canadian Heritage for their financial support through the Canada Council for the Arts, the Canada Book Fund and Livres Canada Books. The publisher also thanks the Government of the Province of British Columbia for the financial support it has given through the Book Publishing Tax Credit program and the British Columbia Arts Council.

 Canada Council for the Arts   Conseil des Arts du Canada   BRITISH COLUMBIA ARTS COUNCIL